# Stan's Song

First published in 2009
by Wayland

This paperback edition published in 2010

Text copyright © Mick Gowar
Illustration copyright © François Hall

Wayland
338 Euston Road
London NW1 3BH

Wayland Australia
Level 17/207 Kent Street
Sydney, NSW 2000

Series Editor: Louise John
Cover design: Paul Cherrill
Design: D.R.ink
Consultant: Shirley Bickler

A CIP catalogue record for this book is available from the British Library.

ISBN 9780750255530 (hbk)
ISBN 9780750255578 (pbk)

Printed in China

Wayland is a division of Hachette Children's Books,
an Hachette Livre UK Company

www.hachettelivre.co.uk

# Stan's Song

Written by Mick Gowar
Illustrated by François Hall

WAYLAND

Sheriff Stan strummed his guitar.
He started to sing.

"A cowboy's best friend is his horse!
Yes, a cowboy's best friend..."

"What are you doing, Sheriff Stan?" asked Deputy Pete.

TOWN
PICNIC
SUNDAY

"I'm practising my singing, Pete," said Sheriff Stan. "I'm playing at the Town Picnic on Sunday."

"Can I play too?" asked Pete.

"Well, what can you play?"
said Stan.

"The drums!" said Pete.

Sheriff Stan sang and played the guitar. Deputy Pete hit the drums.

"Stop, Pete!" shouted Sheriff Stan.
"The drums are too loud. Can you
play anything quieter?"

"Sure thing," said Pete. "I can play the comb and paper."

Sheriff Stan sang and played the guitar. Deputy Pete made buzzing noises on his comb and paper.

"You're just too noisy, Pete," said Stan. "I'll play on my own."

"OK," said Pete sadly.

Sheriff Stan practised hard all week. He sang every song he knew. "A cowboy's best friend is his horse! Yes, a cowboy's best friend..."

"A cowboy's best friend is his dog!
Yes, a cowboy's best friend..."

"A cowboy's best friend is his mouse!
Yes, a cowboy's best friend..."

On Sunday, Stan and Pete went to the picnic. There were cobs of corn, hot dogs and bacon and beans to eat.

Sheriff Stan put down his guitar.
Ma and Dudley Dalton were hiding
behind a tree.

"Let's play a dirty trick on Sheriff
Stan," sniggered Ma Dalton. "Cut
his guitar strings, Dudley. Then he
won't be able to play."

"What with?" asked Dudley.

"These scissors, you big dumbo!"
said Ma.

Twang!

"Oh, no!" said Sheriff Stan.
"My guitar strings are broken!
I can't play."

Suddenly, Stan heard a buzzing sound. Where had he heard that noise before?

Deputy Pete stepped forward. "I've got my comb," he said. "I'll play if you like."

"Thanks, Pete," said Stan. "You're the greatest!"

Pete played the tune on his comb.
Stan hit the back of his guitar like
a drum and sang:

"A cowboy's best friend is...

...his deputy, his deputy!"

And everyone clapped and cheered.
Everyone, that is, except the Daltons!

**START READING** is a series of highly enjoyable books for beginner readers. **The books have been carefully graded to match the Book Bands widely used in schools.** This enables readers to be sure they choose books that match their own reading ability.

## Look out for the Band colour on the book in our Start Reading logo.

The Bands are:

Pink Band 1

Red Band 2

Yellow Band 3

Blue Band 4

Green Band 5

Orange Band 6

Turquoise Band 7

Purple Band 8

Gold Band 9

**START READING** books can be read independently or shared with an adult. They promote the enjoyment of reading through satisfying stories supported by fun illustrations.

**Mick Gowar** has written more than 70 books for children, and likes to visit schools and libraries to give readings and lead workshops. He has also written plays and songs, and has worked with many orchestras. Mick writes his books in a shed in Cambridge.

**François Hall** loves the Wild West, but lives in a terraced 'ranch' down in the South. As well as being quick on the draw, he also designs knitting books. Cowboys often knitted on the homestead and poor Dudley has to wear very itchy underpants made by Ma Dalton!